P9-DZN-255

Marlon Bundo's

A Day in the Life of
THE VICE PRESIDENT

Written by CHARLOTTE PENCE
Illustrated by KAREN PENCE

Regnery Kids

Text copyright © 2018 by Charlotte Pence
Illustrations copyright © 2018 by Karen Pence

All rights reserved. No part of this publication may be reproduced or transmitted in any form
or by any means electronic or mechanical, including photocopy, recording, or any information
storage and retrieval system now known or to be invented, without permission in writing from the
publisher, except by a reviewer who wishes to quote brief passages in connection with a review
written for inclusion in a magazine, newspaper, website, or broadcast.

Regnery Kids™ is a trademark of Salem Communications Holding Corporation;
Regnery® is a registered trademark of Salem Communications Holding Corporation

Cataloging-in-Publication data on file with the Library of Congress

ISBN 978-1-62157-776-8
e-book ISBN 978-1-62157-785-0

Published in the United States by
Regnery Kids, an imprint of
Regnery Publishing
A Division of Salem Media Group
300 New Jersey Ave NW
Washington, DC 20001
www.RegneryKids.com

Published in association with the literary agency of Wolgemuth & Associates, Inc.

Manufactured in the United States of America

10 9 8 7 6 5 4 3 2 1

Books are available in quantity for promotional or premium use.
For information on discounts and terms, please visit our website: www.Regnery.com.

This book is dedicated to our family:
the vice president, Michael, Sarah, and Audrey
for coming with us on this journey,
and to the BOTUS himself,
who represents furry family members across the world
who bring so much joy to our lives.

Allow me to introduce myself—
I am Marlon Bundo Pence.
I live with my family here
At the vice president's residence.

Some people call me BOTUS—
A name any bunny would love.
It means "Bunny of the United States"—
A job I am very proud of!

As the official bunny in residence here,
I help out whenever I can.
So Grampa and I get ready for
The busy day we have planned.

Grampa says goodbye to Grandma,
And we head to the motorcade.
He grabs some freshly brewed coffee
From the Naval Enlisted Aides.

I hop up into the black limo
To make sure I get a good seat.
I want to see all the people
Who will soon be lining the streets!

Each day as we drive to the White House,
We see people waving their flags.
Grampa always gives them a thumbs-up,
And I give my tail a nice wag!

We pull up to the White House West Wing.
This is where the vice president works.
And I hop down the hall to his office
To see which meeting is first.

When I look over Grampa's shoulder,
There's a scene with a familiar feel.
But we're not in Indiana, I know—
It's a painting by T. C. Steele.

Grampa has lots of meetings
And other important events,
But the most important meeting is first.
That's the one with the president!

I love the Oval Office
With its fluffy carpet to walk on.
And I nibble on a carrot,
While Grampa and the president talk on.

Then we race off to the Capitol—
Where Grampa presides over a vote;
He is the president of the Senate,
Which is very important to note.

17

The huge dome is covered with paintings
To the top of the ceiling so high.
The reporters are asking their questions,
And the morning is flying by.

19

Now we drive back toward the White House,
But instead of right, we turn left.
That's where Grampa's second office is—
In the building with lots of steps!

It's the Eisenhower Executive Office Building,
Which is a lot of words to me.
So for short you can call it what I do—
The wonderful EEOB!

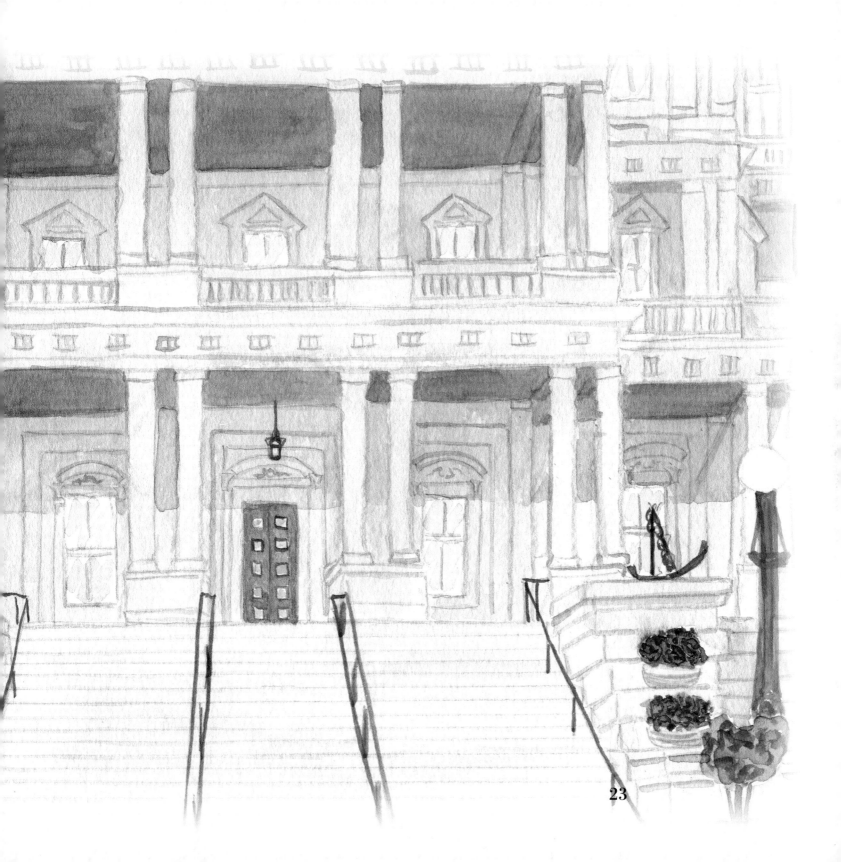

23

We meet people from across America.
I wonder which states they are from.
They come to share stories and questions
and problems,
And Grampa helps answer each one.

When Grampa is done with his meetings,
He walks out the patio doors.
I can see the Washington Monument
And lots of students on tours!

I'm getting awfully tired.

We've sure had a busy day.

So I'm glad we are about to go home.

And maybe we'll have time to play.

We head back to the Naval Observatory

Where we pass through the gates again.

You can tell it's late from the giant clock

With red numbers that read: 8:10.

But we're not quite done with work yet.
We drive up to the top of the street,
And we enter the round-topped building
Where we get a special treat.

Inside there's a giant telescope
Where people can look at the stars.
Grandma picks me up so I can look,
And—I promise—I think I see Mars!

As we go back down to the residence,
I'm very glad to be home.
But as we pass by Grampa's office,
I hear the ringing of the phone.

I tell Grampa his day's not done
By tugging on his shoe.
He picks up the phone—it's the president!
Grampa gives him the day's review.

36

At last Grampa gets out his Bible,
And he quietly bows his head.
I place my paw on his hand
For one little prayer before bed.

I think of all our adventures today,
From the White House to the Capitol dome.
And I remember how blessed I am
To call this great nation my home.

Resources

1. The vice president lives at the vice president's residence, which is at Number One Observatory Circle in Washington, D.C. This means he lives at the Naval Observatory Base. The house was built in 1893 for the superintendent of the Naval Observatory and, in 1974, it became the official residence of the vice president of the United States.

   Walter Mondale was the first vice president to live there, and ever since his term each vice president has lived in the residence with his family. Many administrations have added onto the residence in their own special way. The Bidens built a garden with the names of every family member of past vice presidential families engraved on stones. The Pences added a beehive. Now the residence is also home to over thirty thousand bees!

2. The vice president works every day in the West Wing, where he has his own office down the hall from the president. Inside Vice President Pence's office, he has a painting by the artist T. C. Steele. T. C. Steele is a famous artist from Indiana who is known for painting landscapes of Indiana.

Across the street, the vice president also has a ceremonial office in the Eisenhower Executive Office Building. People who work for the vice president have offices in the West Wing and the EEOB, but most are located in the EEOB.

The ceremonial office is used to host events, receptions, and meetings. The interior decoration was designed by William McPherson. He included symbols of the Navy Department on the walls and ceiling, because the room was originally used by secretaries of the Navy. The vice president's desk in the office is part of the White House Collection and has been signed by each user since the 1940s. From the balcony of the office, a beautiful view of the Washington Monument can be seen in the distance.

3. The vice president also works at the United States Capitol where he meets with legislators to discuss important topics and decisions. He is the official president of the Senate, and sometimes he is called in to preside over a vote. The vice president is also able to vote in the United States Senate, where he can be a "tie-breaker."

4. The vice president speaks to the press and answers questions they may have for him. He has his own "press pool," which is a group of reporters who travel with him when he performs official duties. He holds press conferences in various locations, including the White House and the rotunda, which is the big dome of the Capitol building with historic statues and paintings of our country's history.

5. The property where the vice president's residence sits also has a working Observatory where you can see stars from telescopes. Marlon calls it the "round-topped building," because the top is shaped like a dome. The vice president and Mrs. Pence host events in the Observatory for people to learn more about space. In 2017, they invited children from local schools to watch the solar eclipse at the Observatory.

6. Vice President Pence talks to President Trump on the phone all the time. He is always sure to take time to read his Bible and pray too, as his faith is a very important part of his life.